The Castle

For Jeppe, Jasper and Nora

Albie on His Way
This edition published in 2022 by Red Comet Press LLC, Brooklyn, NY

First published as *Jeppe unterwegs*
Text and art copyright © 2021 Jutta Bauer
Original German edition © Kibitz Verlag
Translation made by arrangement with Am-Book (www.am-book.com)
English translation © 2022 Red Comet Press, LLC
Translated by Matthias Wieland

Library of Congress Control Number: 2022930002
ISBN (HB): 978-1-63655-032-9
ISBN (EBOOK): 978-1-63655-033-6

22 23 24 25 21 26 TLF 10 9 8 7 6 5 4 3 2 1

Manufactured in China

RED COMET PRESS

RedCometPress.com

ALBiE
on his way

JUTTA BAUER

TRANSLATED BY
MATTHIAS WIELAND

RED COMET PRESS · BROOKLYN

One day the king demanded to see me in his castle. Word had reached him that I am quite fast, and he ordered me to deliver an important message to the neighboring king—over the hills, along the river, and then just straight on westward.

I took the scroll with the message and was on my way.

I had just passed the first hill when I had to stop.

Meanwhile at
the castle...

It took a while until Father Squirrel was well enough
that I could continue on my way.

I traveled upriver for several days.
Then I met a very sad little critter.

I ran back down river as fast as I could because I had seen something floating in the water. Then all the way back. The little critter was very pleased.

It was getting dark when I came to a meadow
where I met a very tired mother.

She had to get a few things and
asked if I could keep an eye on the kids.

After a week she came back.
We had a feast.

But I had to be on my way
and said goodbye to the little ones.

I was wandering day and night, making good progress.
The wood was getting darker and denser.
But I felt almost no fear at all.

The next day an old animal was walking ahead of me.
I offered my arm and we walked together for a while.

We were quite slow, though.

At a certain point I said that I wanted
to continue alone and get on my way.

Finally, one fine morning I could spot the neighboring
castle on a hill. Two more days and I'll be there, I rejoiced.

But then, when evening came,
I decided to take a different path.

The other route was terribly long,
and the night was terribly dark and terribly cold.

hop hop

I had to cross icy peaks, deep valleys, and raging rivers.
On a mountaintop my strength finally gave out.

Luckily, a kindly groundhog came my way.
She welcomed me to her home.

It took a while until I fully recovered.

Alma, the groundhog, was very caring.

So, I stayed a little longer.

Finally, I had to be on my way. Just before I reached the castle I took a break and ate Alma's bread with some of Alma's honey.

Then I knocked.
Curiously, the neighboring castle looked exactly like ours . . . only the flowers in the garden were bigger.

??

I was brought to the king. Do all castles around the world have the same carpeting? I was a little worried how the other king might welcome me.

How surprised I was to find my VERY OWN king!

He wasn't angry at all that
I had ended up with him instead
of the neighboring king.

He wanted me to tell
him everything I had
seen along the way.

Whoa!

All through the night I relayed my adventures.
The king marveled at all the people I'd met.

I kept talking and talking, and the king listened intently.

Dawn was breaking when the king
suddenly tossed the scroll into the fire.

Later over breakfast he suggested building
a small house for me on the castle grounds
so I would be around if something came up.

He ordered some timber
and we started building right away.

When we were finished,
the king sent a message to Alma,
inviting her to move in with me.

Whenever we had pumpkins to harvest,
all our friends would come to help.

Father Squirrel and his family visited quite regularly.

Jutta Bauer is one of Germany's best-known children's book creators. She is the recipient of the prestigious Hans Christian Andersen Medal for her "lasting contribution" as a children's book illustrator. Jutta Bauer lives in her native city of Hamburg, Germany. **jutta-bauer.info**

Albie's Path

Albie slept here

The Old Animal

The River

The Squirrel Tree